This book belongs to

....

....

Useful words

(in the order they appear in this book)

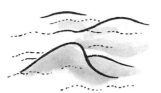

sand

sea

beach

sandcastle

sunhat

Grey letters represent silent letters.

Sammy Snake's Day at the Seaside

Lyn Wendon

"Let's go to the seaside,"
said Sammy Snake to his
sister Sally.

"It's such a nice sunny day."

"Oooh, yesss," hissed Sally.

"I love to play in the sand

and swim in the sea."

So Sammy and Sally Snake set off for the sea. Soon they came to a splendid stretch of beach.

"Let's make a sandcastle,"
said Sally Snake.

"Oooh, yess," hissed Sammy.

Both snakes worked very hard. At last the sandcastle was finished.

"It's a super sandcastle,"
hissed Sammy. "Now let's go
for a swim."

"Oooh, yes," hissed Sally.
They swam and swam until
their skins got too salty.

"Now let's play Hide and Seek," said Sally.

"I'm too sleepy," said Sammy Snake.

"You can have the first turn to hide," said Sally.

So Sammy set off to find somewhere to hide. He soon found the perfect spot – under somebody's sunhat lying on the sand.

Sally counted slowly up to twenty.

"Sssixteen, ssseventeen, eighteen, nineteen, **twenty**," she said, opening her eyes.

... 16, 17, 18, 19...

Sally looked and looked but she could not find Sammy. Suddenly she heard a soft snoring sound.

"Sssammy!" she hissed.

"Ssstop sssleeping! We're

supposed to be playing

Hide and Seek... not

Hide and Sleep!"

The Letterlanders

Annie Apple   **Bouncy Ben**   **Clever Cat**   **Dippy Duck**   **Eddy Elephant**   **Fireman Fred**   **Golden Girl**

Hairy Hat Man   **Impy Ink**   **Jumping Jim**   **Kicking King**   **Lucy Lamp Lady**   **Munching Mike**

Naughty Nick   **Oscar Orange**   **Poor Peter**   **Quarrelsome Queen**   **Robber Red**   **Sammy Snake**   **Ticking Tess**

Uppy Umbrella   **Vase of Violets**   **Wicked Water Witch**   **Max and Maxine**   **Yo-yo Man**   **Zig Zag Zebra**

This edition produced for
The Book People Ltd., Hall Wood Avenue,
Haydock, St. Helens WA11 9UL

Published by Collins Educational
An imprint of HarperCollins*Publishers* Ltd
77-85 Fulham Palace Road
London W6 8JB

The HarperCollins website address is
www.**fire**and**water**.com

For non-UK supplies please refer to:
Letterland International Ltd, Barton, Cambridge CB3 7AY, UK
email: sales@letterland.com

www.letterland.com

© **Lyn Wendon 1999**
First published 1998
Reprinted, 1998, 2000

ISBN 0 00 303437 2

LETTERLAND® is a registered trademark of Lyn Wendon.

British Library Cataloguing in Publication Data
A catalogue record for this book is available from the British Library.

Written by Lyn Wendon
Illustrated by Anna Jupp
Designed by Michael Sturley
Consultant: Lyn Wendon, originator of Letterland

Printed by Printing Express, Hong Kong